I0624666

KINDLING FRIENDSHIPS

By

VERONICA A. PURCELL

Kindling Friendships

Print Edition
Copyright © 2015 Veronica A. Purcell
The moral right of the author has been asserted.

This book is licensed for your personal enjoyment only. All rights reserved, including the right to reproduce this book, or a portion thereof, in any form except for the use of brief quotations in articles or reviews. This book may not be resold or uploaded for distribution to others.

This is a work of fiction. References to real people, events, establishments, organizations, distilleries or locales are intended only to provide a sense of authenticity, and are used fictitiously. All other characters, and all incidents and dialogue, are drawn from the author's imagination and are not to be construed as real.

Cover Design: Robin Bourque
Cover Photos: Charles Doucet
ISBN-978-0-994048905

ROYAL OAKS
PUBLISHING

DEDICATION

To Gerry,
my real life hero.

ACKNOWLEDGEMENTS

To Tom and Janet Davis for their friendship and support. I wish everyone had the good fortune to have neighbors like them.

To my family and friends who read my manuscript, thank you for your encouragement and suggestions.

To Mike and his team at SystemCare, thanks for all you did to get me back home again.

To the Pleasantville Fire Department and surrounding fire departments for all their efforts to save my home.

To my editor, Pat Thomas for helping me turn an idea into a story.

KINDLING FRIENDSHIPS

It's funny how my brain makes sense of information that it collects – mine made all sorts of crazy connections when I heard the strange sounds coming from the mudroom that evening. They distracted me from the conversation I wanted to have with my new neighbours because I couldn't figure out what was causing them.

At first, I thought the popping noises were from something in the oven, but I dismissed that idea because I wasn't cooking anything. Then, I had the bizarre idea that it was icicles falling off the eaves trough onto the ground. Finally, when I'd exhausted all the explanations that flitted through my mind, I got up to investigate.

You need to know I'm from Toronto, Ontario. Born and bred there. It's where all the members of my family live, including my children and grandchildren. Knowing that, you might wonder why I am living here on the South Shore of Nova Scotia.

It's because of my husband, Alan. He's an East Coast boy. It was always his dream to come home to the South Shore of Nova Scotia. So, when the opportunity to buy his parents' home came along, we didn't jump at the chance. At least I didn't. Don't get me wrong, I love Nova Scotia and I understand why Rita MacNeil sang, "There's just so much beauty the heart can't believe." Nova Scotia has all that.

But moving meant ending my career, uprooting my whole life. It was a very big decision. I thought about the space, the peace and quiet, and the more relaxed pace of life in Nova Scotia. I smiled at the thought of drinking my morning cup of tea out on the back deck overlooking the LaHave River. Romanticizing it, I could visualize the quaint, white-steepled church that was across the river from us and I remembered the restful sound of the wind rustling the leaves of two enormous "Royal Oak" trees standing on the front lawn. The story is that they grew from acorns that Alan's ancestors took from the Sandringham Estate: The Norfolk retreat of HM The Queen, during the Second World War. Compared to the crowded, hectic City of Toronto, the South Shore seemed like heaven. In the city, I spent most of my time sitting on a highway that felt more like a parking lot. I felt like there were never enough hours in a day to get everything done and sleep was a luxury.

The idea of moving was all nice and good, but money is what actually won me over. The place was beautiful, a great value, and I knew we could never afford a beautiful house on the water in Toronto. So, we packed up what we thought would fit our new lifestyle and gave the rest of our belongings away.

The plan we came up with wasn't perfect. Not by a long shot. Because of my age and the years I'd put into teaching, I was able to retire from my job as a teacher, but Alan, wasn't quite in the same position. He has his own consulting firm so although he could occasionally work from home, it was a bit of a struggle to set up a schedule that allowed him to work from Nova Scotia. His job still required him to be in Toronto quite a bit. Consequently, once we did move, I was left on my own more than I anticipated.

Alan and I had big plans for an elaborate extension to the back of the house as well as remodelling the kitchen and bathroom, but those things would have to wait. Being responsible with money got in the way of my best renovation ideas.

I filled my time decorating our new home. I did most of the work myself. One time I wanted to surprise Alan so I stayed up late into the night for two weeks straight so that I could get the main floor painted before he came home. I found a handyman to install crown mouldings and paint the two-story entryway. I moved the furniture around a few times trying to decide on just the right place for my sofa with the lovely William Morris fabric. *Should it face opposite the main entry from the centre hall or sit under the windows facing off the front porch?*

I was proud of the changes, all undertaken with minimal expense and a lot of sweat equity. I stood in the doorways, admiring how the beautiful old rooms showcased my city furniture, and vice versa.

Alan's homestead began to feel like home. But even that wasn't enough. I'd left more than a home behind in Toronto. I wanted more than a home here. I wanted a circle of friends.

When Alan's parents moved out of the family home, they bought a smaller house in town. They were thrilled by the changes we were making to the family home. Finally, after many, many years, one of their children had come back home. I don't think it mattered to them what we did to the house, as long as we were happy to be there. They were so kind and often invited me for dinner, or drove me around the area, visiting local attractions – but it wasn't the same as having friends of my own.

One of the bribes that Alan had used to convince me to move was to agree to buy a dog. I love dogs while Alan likes other people's dogs. To me, it made perfect sense to buy a dog. I was alone in the house so much, that I felt having a dog was protection as well as company. And best of all, I knew having a dog was a great way to meet people. So, Griffyn, a black standard poodle entered our lives.

I found out the best dog walking place in the area was a stretch of sandy beach shaped like a crescent. I would pack an excited Griffyn in the car and off we'd go. Sure enough, there were lots of dogs and their owners. Griffyn and I went for our daily walk in all kinds of weather, at low tide or high tide. We didn't care.

I varied my walking times to meet as many people as I could. Often, they were already in well-established groups – both dogs and people. I got to know many of the dogs by name and a few of the owners, but once we left the beach, I was friendless once again.

I attended all sorts of community breakfasts, suppers and bazaars. If Alan was in town he joined me, otherwise, I went on my own. I even became adept at going to movies by myself. There was never a problem finding a seat for one and I would slip in just before the movie began so it wouldn't be so obvious that I was by myself. Early on, I made the mistake of showing up well before the movie started. I sat in the well-lit movie theatre by myself, waiting for darkness to fall... to hide the fact that I was alone. I was sure the whole place could see that I was by myself. The only upside was I didn't have to share my popcorn.

I made regular phone calls to my children. Yes, old-fashioned phone calls because texting wasn't an option. The cell reception inside our house was non-existent when we moved in. We finally figured out that if we wanted to get our cell phone to work we needed to go down to the deck and hang out over the river to get a signal. The biggest fear was that I could drop my phone in the water while I dialled.

So I was alone and felt disconnected a lot. And it was worse when my neighbours across the street put the for sale sign on their lawn. I hadn't known they planned to move until the sign went up because they kept their distance and had become "just the people that lived across the street," not really the kind of neighbours that welcomed a "Come From Away."

Regardless of the reason, I was lonely.

My friends and family regularly tossed

out the idea that they'd be coming down for a visit, but in those first couple years, no one ever did. That was why, on some level, I was actually excited to see the SOLD sign on the house across the street that fall. The place had been for sale for at least two years. I didn't want to get my hopes up, but I wished someone like me would move in, someone from away. I knew it was unlikely that the people who bought the house would be new to the neighbourhood because many people in the area were long-time residents – complete with family and long-established friendships. The buyers were probably the son or daughter of someone down the road. But maybe, just maybe, these people would be more like me. I hoped that was possible.

It was December when I met my new neighbours, Jane and Stephen. By chance, we ended up sitting across from each other at the Community Fire Hall's Christmas potluck dinner. My husband, Alan, was in Toronto. I was there with my in-laws. It was actually my mother-in-law, Faye, who met them first.

Faye is about as outgoing as a bee in a

flower garden in full bloom. She will talk to everyone and anyone. I remember one time she even started a conversation with people who were standing in line waiting to pay at a particularly temperamental parking lot ticket machine in Halifax. By the time it was our turn to pay, we knew all about their plans for their day in the city. So, true to form, before we even got up for our turn at the buffet table she had found out that Jane and Stephen were my new neighbours.

She'd also learned that Jane was a semi-retired lawyer from Halifax and Stephen, a retired engineer from Ontario. It took her only a few more questions and we knew they had decided to start married life together in the house across the street from me. Both of them were new residents to the South Shore. Just like me. And, both had children living in Ontario. Just like me.

Through the course of the evening I found out that we had more things in common. One of them was that Jane and I wanted to take painting lessons now that we had the time. I offered to drop by their home when I got some information about upcoming painting classes.

The drive home from the Community dinner felt different – a kind of good I hadn't felt in a long time. As soon as I arrived home, I switched on my computer and researched painting classes. Then, I called Alan to let him know about our new neighbours. He pretended to be just as excited by the news as I was.

It was Christmas and Jane and Stephen's children had made the trip from Ontario to visit them so I planned to wait until after the main festivities were over before I told her what I'd learned. We hadn't exchanged phone numbers, so I was going to visit in person and show her the schedule for painting classes.

One evening, I saw the lights on in their front room through the bare branches of the trees that separated our homes and decided to drop over. Although Christmas was over, I knew some of their family were still visiting, but I decided that enough time had passed that my visit wouldn't be too intrusive. Jane was pleased to see me and offered me a glass of wine.

Wine drinkers. Another thing we have in common. I spent a pleasant hour drinking wine with Jane and her daughters and making plans to register us for the upcoming art class in Chester. As I was leaving, I had the brilliant idea to invite her and Stephen over for drinks once Alan came back from Toronto. She grabbed her calendar and we set a date for just after New Year's Day.

When I walked home that evening, I felt my spirits lift. I had spent time relaxing with a friend. It was the first time, since I had moved to the South Shore, that I truly felt like I belonged in Nova Scotia.

I was anxious for our evening to go well. Jane and Stephen were coming over for the first time. I spoke to my daughter earlier that day about my excitement at hosting an evening with my new friends. She cautioned me not to overwhelm them with my enthusiasm.

I spent the day over-cleaning (if such a

thing is possible), making shortbread cookies and agonizing over selecting just the right wine. As a final touch, I placed a bowl of spicy, pink, chocolate-filled Chicken Bones in the living room to be nibbled on as the evening progressed. The dining room table was laid out with a variety of snacks. My best china and seasonal napkins were artistically placed at an angle on the table to be used later in the evening.

The main entrance to our home was actually through the back door. I wanted the first impression of my home to be a good one so I made sure the mudroom was perfect. I removed several of my husband's coats to make room for our guests' outerwear and hung my things on the row of hooks beside the French door leading to the kitchen. Every boot and shoe was lined up ready for company. Just the day before, I'd spent two hours searching the post-season clearance tables to find just the right pair of boots. I was excited about my new Riekers and I couldn't wait to wear them. I placed them front and centre on the shoe rack as a matter of pride.

I even polished the glass starfish,

bought in the summer at a craft shop in Lunenburg. I placed it on the windowsill to highlight how perfectly its colours matched the blue in the walls. The nightlight that was plugged into the outlet by the kitchen door cast a welcoming rainbow through the window by the back door.

Although everything was ready, I was so anxious that I couldn't sit and relax. Instead, I spent the last few minutes before their arrival, giving Griffyn a quick brushing. I also debated with my husband about picking out just the right tie for the occasion, but my husband persuaded me that having the dog wear a tie might be a bit over the top. *What can I say?*

I knew that I was going a little overboard, but I couldn't help myself. Making a good impression and creating a memorable evening for our guests that night was very important to me.

So, drinks had been served and the evening was going better than I had hoped. Alan and Stephen planned a golf game as soon as the snow melted. Jane and I decided to take turns driving to the painting classes. Clearly,

Griffyn approved of our new friends because he was curled up at Stephen's feet. I sat back and relaxed, enjoying the conversation. That's when I heard the strange sounds and reluctantly excused myself to investigate.

As I crossed the front hallway and entered the kitchen, I was completely unprepared for what I found.

Giant red and orange flames leaped against the panes of glass at the French door separating the kitchen from the mudroom. The flames were so big they touched the ceiling. From where I stood, it looked like the entire mudroom was an inferno. Smoke snaked its way into the kitchen, seeping underneath and through cracks in the doorway.

The noise that had initially drawn me into the room was now louder and more persistent. I realized that it was the windows in the mudroom shattering, one by one, under the intense heat. The coats, shoes and boots that only a short time ago had been hung neatly on their hooks or sat on shelves or in baskets now fed the fire that regurgitated our winter outerwear as noxious, black smoke.

I watched as the fire's mad dance transformed into a full-out attack on the door – the only barrier that kept the flames from the rest of our home.

I screamed, "Oh my God! *My house is on fire!*" I know that isn't very original, but I felt that it conveyed the right sense of urgency to the others.

My husband and guests hadn't heard the strange sounds that had caused me to leave and they were still in the living room making polite conversation and casually sipping their drinks. Clearly, my scream hadn't quite prepared them for what was happening because they didn't run. Instead, they calmly put their drinks down and leisurely rounded the corner into the kitchen. There was stunned silence as they took in the situation.

Jane later confessed to me that she got the impression I could be a drama queen, and had expected to see nothing more than flames from a pot boiling over on the stove – I don't know how she got the idea that I could be a little over the top.

It took only seconds for the initial shock of the situation to wear off, and my husband leaped into action. His only thought was to save his family home while he still had a chance. He opened the door to the mudroom to fight the fire but it was like the smoke had been waiting for the opportunity. The black wave that had been held back, exploded into the kitchen. My eyes began to water from all the smoke. I looked across the room at my husband, so close to the fire that the giant flames illuminated his face. He shouted for me to get the fire extinguisher.

I froze. *Fire extinguisher?* Where was it?

Alan rushed past me to grab something to fill with water and he grabbed the first thing he could find – the pan I use to soak my feet. As he passed me, I remembered where I had stored the fire extinguisher and hurried to grab it while my husband pushed past me again, this time to refill his bowl.

Now, in a crisis you don't have time to experiment, you act – or you don't. It might not have been the best course of action, but I was not thinking clearly at the time. My house was on fire; my husband was throwing bowls of water on the flames; and I believed it was my duty to jump in and help. So that is what I did.

I'd never used a fire extinguisher before, so I fumbled around trying to figure out how to make it work. I remembered that there was a ring to pull and then you were supposed to squeeze the trigger. So, I pulled out the ring and squeezed – sort of aiming at the fire. In hindsight, I was too far away to actually do much good, but it wasn't the distance away from the fire that was the big problem. The real issue was that I pointed the fire extinguisher in the wrong direction.

I sprayed it right in my face. Worse, is that I had so much adrenaline rushing through me that I hardly noticed. I simply turned it around and valiantly attempted to spray what was left in the general direction of the fire. By that time, it didn't help at all. I was frantic. I was certain we were going to lose our home.

Even though he barely knew us, Stephen bravely joined Alan in the mudroom.

He grabbed smoldering pieces of footwear and coats and tossed them out the back door into the snow. Meanwhile, Alan ran back and forth with bowls of water to throw on the fire. Because we kept opening the door to fight the fire or throw things outside, the smoke was drawn inward and was engulfing the kitchen.

It was unbelievable how quickly the room filled with the black, acrid cloud. Within moments, the air around us was so thick and dark that you could barely see. Jane, who calmly watched the rest of us rush around, realized that the house was dangerously full of smoke. Her quick assessment of the situation was that it was no longer safe for us to be in there. She suggested that we get out of the house. Quickly. Then she asked me where Griffyn was.

I peered through the dense smoke, trying to find him. My panic level went up about ten notches when I realized he wasn't with us. I called his name, but I wasn't certain he would respond in all the panic and confusion. I couldn't believe it when he immediately appeared through the smoke and headed toward us. He'd been hiding in the sunroom where the smoke was the worst. He would have been trapped if we hadn't called him.

I grabbed him tightly by the collar, relieved that at least he was safe. We left Alan and Stephen to fight the fire and made our way through the smoke-filled rooms and out the front door into the freezing cold. In our panic to get out of the house and with Alan's and Stephen's focused attempts to put out the fire, none of us stopped to call 911.

The snow had been falling in earnest during the early afternoon and now it was hard to distinguish the front lawns from the road. Cold gusts of wind swirled the snow into white clouds that could be seen in the green and red Christmas lights that outlined the neighbour's porch railings and shrubs. The snow was piled so high that it covered the front steps – our only means of escape.

The shrill ring of our smoke alarm bounced off the falling snow and echoed eerily in the night. Jane and I stood on the front porch gulping in breaths of clean, frosty air. I was in my slippers and Jane was in her stocking feet.

The cold air must have activated Jane's common sense because she turned to me and said, "Anne, we need to call 911."

Her words propelled me into another impulsive action. Obviously, my common sense was somewhere buried deep inside, under the panic and bone-chilling cold. Without stopping to think, I turned around and rushed right back into the house. I hurried past the cordless phone that was just inside the front door and into the kitchen to get my cell phone – yes, I ran right into the place where the smoke was thickest.

My phone was on the table, near the source of the fire. I grabbed it off the kitchen table and raced back outside.

I was in such a state that it didn't even dawn on me until after I was outside that going in for my cell phone had been a bad idea, for two reasons: One, I put myself in grave danger when I went back into a burning building and two, there is very poor cell reception so why had I bothered? I guess I didn't know if the house phone would still be working. But instead of taking a chance on the cordless house phone, I was now clutching an almost useless cell phone in my frozen hands.

My fingers were fumbling, more from panic than from cold, as I tried to dial 911. Surprisingly, I got a brief connection, one that was long enough to let emergency know there was a problem, but not long enough to identify myself and our location. I learned later that the RCMP can track the location of 911 calls.

As I tried to redial, I saw Stephen running toward us, down our snow-covered, icy driveway – in his stocking feet. He was yelling something about getting another fire extinguisher. As he rounded the shrubbery that divided our property from the property next door he fell and he hit the ground hard. It looked painful from where we were standing.

To give him credit, he was only down for a moment; then he was back up, clutching his elbow and running toward our other neighbours' house.

From our vantage point on the front porch, Jane and I could see my next door neighbours, Sue and Fred, peering out their side window. I guess the sound of the smoke alarm alerted them to the fact that something unusual was happening next door. We watched Stephen as he alternated between waving his arms at them and rubbing his elbow.

He shouted at them to call 911. It was clear that they didn't understand what he was saying through their windows because, instead of leaping into action, they stood frozen in place. But, Stephen is not a quitter. The fact that his message wasn't being received didn't faze him. He continued on his mission, disappearing around the corner of their house, headed for their door.

Seeing Stephen going for help made me feel guilty for just standing there on the front porch doing nothing. Then it hit me: I would follow Stephen's lead. Our neighbour across the street was the Deputy Fire Marshall. I would go to his place.

Before I headed off, I asked Jane to hold on to Griffyn. She was reluctant at first. She wasn't sure Griffyn would be happy to wait with a woman he had just met. I left him with her and disappeared into the snowstorm. I assured her that my fifty-five pound dog would do exactly as he was told. I didn't tell her he had needed, not one, but three complete series of obedience classes and even then, this investment in time and effort was often not obvious in his behaviour. Usually, he follows commands only if treats are involved.

I crossed my fingers that he would actually obey. Then, leaving the two of them on our front porch, I made my way down the uneven, snow-covered stones that acted as the front stairs.

I slipped and slithered through the deepening snow toward the Deputy Fire Marshall's home. Once I had safely crossed the street, I carefully made my way up his steep driveway. While I walked over to his house, I kept trying to call 911 on my cell phone. The call connected just as I rang his doorbell.

The house looked dark as I peered through the front door window. After all the trouble of getting here, I worried he wasn't home.

As I waited there for the door to open, I could feel my heart pounding. I was coughing from the smoke I had inhaled, my slippers were full of snow and I couldn't feel my toes. I think I was too full of adrenaline to realize that I had very little protection from the bitter wind, dressed as I was in my thin, gold-threaded Christmas blouse and non-creasing, black dress pants.

But all of a sudden, none of that mattered. My emergency phone call was answered: I was connected to a voice. There was actually someone at the other end of the line and they were going to come to our rescue! The conversation went something like this:

"My house is on fire."

"Is everyone out of the house?"

"Yes." I couldn't imagine that my husband would still be in the house alone, fighting the fire.

"What is your address?"

Just as I was completing the emergency call my neighbour answered the door. He started to say a calm hello but my shrill and rather hysterical announcement that my house was on fire, quickly changed his demeanour.

It was amazing to watch the transformation. One minute he was casually leaning against the door and then, mere seconds later, he was rushing down his hallway to put on his Firefighting gear. He hadn't even closed his front door.

Mission accomplished, I turned and headed back toward our home. I could hear our ominous smoke alarm calling to me through the snowstorm. But I had achieved my goal to get assistance. Help was on its way. All the work I had just done on the house was going to be saved. Everything would be okay. That's what I told myself...

Little did I know the evening's events weren't close to being resolved. Reaching those neighbour's had lulled me into a false sense of security. In my defense, I felt that I had done my all, that my attention was no longer needed to help fight the fire and now I was free to move on. To share my pain. So, before I had even reached the road, and true to form, I felt the need to call someone, to tell them about our crisis, as if somehow sharing all this would help.

I chose to call Alan's parents who lived in town, about a fifteen-minute drive from us in good weather. I didn't think about the fact that my cell phone had a Toronto 416 area code which might confuse them. I didn't think about the fact that the cell reception is sporadic and only the worst parts of my conversation might be heard. I didn't think about the fact that it was now snowing quite hard and that I was in slippers walking down an unfamiliar driveway in the dark trying to dial a phone with shaking fingers.

Surprisingly, I got through. No problem at all. Later I learned my mother-in-law had understood enough of the phone call to recognize that it was someone from Toronto calling and they had a terrible cough and they seemed to be in trouble. She couldn't figure out why they were calling her.

It was at this point, as I was trying to

make myself understood that I suffered my first true injury of the evening. Take it from me, walking and talking during a snowstorm, in slippers, down an unfamiliar path is not a good idea. I'd turned back toward my house and somehow lost my footing as I rushed to get there. I stumbled over an icy mound of snow – you know, the rock-solid kind of lump that is left like concrete pylons, marking the edges of a driveway after it's plowed.

My slippers were no protection against the hard chunks of ice. I felt my practically unprotected toes smash into the mound of ice and lost my balance. I fell over the top of the embankment and down the other side, sliding on my stomach over a patch of ice. And no surprise – the phone flew from my hands.

I fumbled around for a few minutes in the snow trying to find my phone. Luckily the only thing that was really hurt was my pride. I took my tumble as a sign that I should re-think sharing my pain. I retrieved my phone and gave up making any more calls to family and friends. Instead, I slowed down, focused and limped back across the street to where Griffyn and Jane waited.

Once again, my dog surprised me. He had sat quietly beside Jane the whole time – Without any treats to bribe him to good behaviour. Poor Jane had been worrying the whole time I was gone that if my dog took it into his head to go after me, there was no way that she could stop him. I've often heard news stories that show in times of crisis, kids and pets can rise to the occasion and Griffyn, perfectly obedient that night, had demonstrated that. I was so proud of him!

It was hard to believe that it had been only a matter of minutes since we had discovered the fire. When I reached her, Jane had no idea what had happened to Alan and Stephen. We had seen Stephen go to the neighbours', but Jane wasn't sure if he was still there. Surely Alan wouldn't still be in the burning house? Not in that smoke. I told the emergency operator the house was empty.
Now, because I couldn't see him, I wasn't so sure.

Jane convinced me that he was fine and that the best way to help was for us to get somewhere safe. We needed to cross the street to her house.

I hated to leave before I was sure Alan was safe. Deep down I knew that going up the dark driveway and around to the back of a burning building to check on him didn't make sense. It was treacherous.

He had seen us leave and probably thought we were already over at Jane's safe and warm…

But what if he's hurt?

Jane stood there shivering, watching me trying to decide what to do. Gently, she took hold of my hand and pulled me toward the stairs.

"Stephen would never have left if Alan was still in the building. I'm sure he is outside waiting for help to arrive." That convinced me. Reluctantly, I grabbed Griffyn by the collar and we followed Jane's lead down the stairs. Really, we had no other choice.

We made it to Stephen and Jane's place and the first thing Jane did was to turn up the heat. The second thing she did was put the kettle on to boil. I turned the chairs in the living room around so that I could sit and look

29

out the window across the road to our house.

Griffyn sniffed around, checking out all the new smells. He had a hard time settling down and came over to me every few minutes for a reassuring pat on the head. When I bent down to give him a hug, my nose filled with the smell of my fire-ravaged home. That's when the reality hit. Our lovely home was in danger, the one I'd worked so hard to make comfortable, and where my husband had grown up.

I held Griffyn tightly trying hard not to cry. I hadn't shed a tear till then and I was afraid if I started, I wouldn't be able to stop.

The kettle hadn't even begun to boil before we saw the fire trucks and ambulance pull up with their lights flashing and sirens blazing. Even an RCMP vehicle navigated the deep snow and plowed its way up our driveway. We watched and waited, and our toes began to thaw. Soon my injured toe began to throb, but I felt too foolish to tell Jane how I'd hurt it.

As Jane and I watched the activity happening across the street we counted our blessings. Privately, I prayed that Jane had been right and Alan was safe. We were lucky. Things could have been much worse.

"Could you imagine the damage if you hadn't been home?" said Jane.

"Or, if we had been upstairs sleeping?" I countered and then I added, "or, if Griffyn had been home alone?"

That was one of the worst. It put a stop to our imagined scenarios. We both turned back to look out the window. Silently, we watched as flakes of snow blanketed the emergency vehicles parked in front of my home.

There was still no sign of Alan or Stephen. What was keeping them? Neither Jane nor I voiced our concerns out loud. We sipped our tea, acting as if everything would be okay. I guess that is how we managed to cope.

Eventually, the ambulance left, along with all but one of the fire trucks. Soon after, Stephen arrived, still in his stocking feet. I watched as Jane gave him a big hug. Griffyn jumped up and down, circling the couple.

Then Griffyn went to the door, as if expecting Alan. But nobody else came.

Stephen told us my next door neighbours didn't have a fire extinguisher to borrow, but they did provide him with a dry pair of socks which by now were soaking wet. He'd singed off his eyebrows and his elbow was bruised from the fall on the driveway, but otherwise he was unhurt.

The fire was out, Stephen explained, but a few firemen were still in the house, checking, making sure there was no fire in our walls. He had last seen Alan at the back of our house, but hadn't seen him since.

He could tell by the look on my face that it wasn't what I wanted to hear. Then Jane and

Stephen both assured me that he was safe – *but they didn't know for sure, did they?*

The worst part of the evening was the time after that, waiting for Alan to arrive. As the minutes crawled by I became more and more anxious. Griffyn must have sensed my mood because he wouldn't settle. He kept going back and forth between the door and where I sat. The red lights of the remaining fire truck flashed through the windows at regular intervals. The four of us waited anxiously for Alan to walk up the driveway.

Stephen tried to keep my mind off Alan by showing me funny clips from the Internet. He even set up his laptop on the table beside me and said, "Have you heard of these guys from Ireland? They are hilarious. You've got to see this clip."

The comedic skit had a kind of Monty Python feel to it. Although I wasn't really in the mood to laugh, it did drag my attention away from the flashing lights across the street.

Eventually, the sole fire truck left and only the streetlight illuminated the snow surrounding us. I took it as a good sign. The fire must be out. But what was keeping Alan?

The wind had stopped blowing and the snow looked like a white sheet stretching from Stephen and Jane's home across the street to our front porch. The tire marks from the emergency vehicles looked like creases in the otherwise smooth surface. It was so late that the neighbours had turned off their Christmas lights and Griffyn had finally fallen asleep with his head resting on my feet. I watched his chest silently rise and fall, willing myself to match my breathing to his in an effort to keep myself calm.

Finally, we saw a lone figure make its way up the driveway. Griffyn was awake in an instant. He rushed to the door. His tail was wagging to hard the whole back half of his body was moving from side to side. He only beat me to the door by seconds. Alan didn't even get a chance to close the door before I had wrapped my arms around him. Griffyn bounced around the two of us like a kernel of popcorn in a hot air popper.

Alan's forehead was burned and his clothes reeked of smoke, but he was all right. He had his computer with him but no coat, no scarf and no winter boots.

Our vigil at the front window was over. We all sank gratefully into big, comfortable chairs. We never gave a thought to the smoke seeping from our clothes into the upholstery. We were just glad to let the tension ease from our bodies. Sipping from large glasses of wine, we replayed scenes from the evening over and over.

Alan told us that just before the fire trucks arrived he'd thrown enough water on the fire to get it out. His heroic efforts had stopped the fire from engulfing the rest of our home. He stayed with the firemen as they tore holes in our kitchen walls to make sure that the fire had not made its way through them and up to the second floor. He also met with the RCMP who'd been alerted by my phone call.

We all sat there coughing because our lungs were raw from the smoke, and drinking wine until the adrenaline stopped pumping. Then exhaustion set in. Jane and Stephen showed us up to their guest room and told Alan and me we were welcome to stay as long as we needed. Griffyn usually slept downstairs not with us. Tonight we made an exception. He curled up on the floor beside the bed and quickly dozed off. I was exhausted, but I couldn't fall asleep. I listened to Alan coughing. Each deep burst sounded like his lungs were scraped raw from all the smoke he'd inhaled. No matter which way I turned my head I could still smell smoke.

It was a celebratory breakfast the next morning. We lingered over scrambled eggs, homemade jam and hot coffee. Stephen looked comical with his singed eyebrows and Alan's whole body shook as he coughed every few minutes, but at least everyone was safe. I was sure that I was going to lose a toenail, but if that was the worst, we could count ourselves lucky.

The telephone rang, interrupting our hundredth going over of the previous night's events. It was the insurance company. Alan had contacted the emergency number before we'd gone to bed. Someone from a fire restoration company was coming out to the house this morning. Could we meet them?

We borrowed coats and boots from Stephen and Jane and trudged through the snow to our house across the street. Everything looked pristine as we approached the front. Then, we followed the curve of the driveway to what had been our back door. Just outside the entrance to our home was a mound of frozen, blackened boots and shoes covered in new white snow.

Seeing that should have prepared me for what waited inside, but it didn't.

Alan pushed open the twisted door. The ceiling of the mudroom was gone. In its place were blackened rafters. A wire hung where the ceiling light had been. All that was left of the windows were shards of glass embedded in the once-white window frames. There was no evidence of the rainbow nightlight. The electrical outlet it had been plugged into was just a twisted metal box. The cover was missing, and exposed wires stretched toward us like tentacles. The floor was a charred mess too. As we pushed open what was left of the

French door to the kitchen our feet crunched on the frozen bits that had once been the walls.

Inside, rivulets stained black with smoke made long streaks down the walls that I had painted a month ago. The new crown moulding was cracked and the brand new carpet was covered in soot. The coffee table still held the wine glasses from the evening before, but they were surrounded by a layer of ashes. The wind was blowing through our windowless mudroom and we soon discovered the electricity wasn't working in the back part of the house.

All my hours of hard work were wasted. My house would never be the same. I hadn't expected the damage to be so extensive. I was devastated. What had, only hours ago, been a bright and cheerful home was now a dark, cold, unwelcoming place.

While Alan met with the representative from the fire restoration company, I wandered through the house. As I saw more and more of the damage the fire had wrought, I became overwhelmed. I returned to the mudroom and found a pile of mismatched boots and shoes. These were what had been missed in all the chaos. Their partners were outside in the frozen pile by the back door. Some were covered in bits of glass and soot, so I used my toe and nudged the pile of stiff footwear.

It's funny what becomes important at times like this.

I pushed aside various shoes, sandals and boots in search of my brand new Riekers. I was obsessed with finding my boots. If I could find them, then all was not lost. I bent down and started to use my hands. I didn't care about the glass. I needed to find my boots.

Finally, I spied the toe of one boot and pushed aside the rubble to unearth that one. *But where was the other?* Surely it had to be close by. How could one boot survive and the other not? I searched the same pile again, hoping for a different result.

Then I remembered the pile of frozen footwear outside the back door. I rushed outside and furiously kicked away at the frozen mound. My new boots, lost. Kick. My beautiful home, ruined. Kick. All my hard work, gone. Kick. Even with all my kicking, I barely chipped away a few pieces of ice from the rock-solid pile.

My frustrated attempts triggered the tears I had been holding back. Crying hysterically, I flung the one boot I had found as far as I could. I watched it spin in the air, making a soft *plop* as it landed in the deep snow.

Something must have alerted Alan to the fact that there was a problem. Perhaps it was hearing his wife yelling and angrily kicking the pile of frozen boots outside by the back door.

"Anne, what are you doing?" Alan asked as he joined me.

It seemed pretty obvious to me, but I replied, "Looking for my boot. It has to be here."

"Which one?"

I was filled with anger at having lost so much. I couldn't answer him. Instead I stomped through the snow and retrieved the boot. "These ones." I held it up for his inspection. "I could only find one. The other has to be here somewhere."

He didn't say anything. He just turned around and went back inside. I returned to kicking the pile of frozen footwear. Moments later he stepped outside. The mate to my Rieker boot was in his hand. Somehow it had been buried under some rubble on the other side of the mudroom away from the rest of the footwear. He smiled and handed me the boot. I looked at him and then back at my boots. Maybe there was hope after all.

I followed Alan back into the house. Two huge HEPA fans had been set up by the man from the fire restoration company. I went upstairs and gathered a few belongings while the guy went over some details with Alan. By the time I returned he was gone and the house was quiet except for the hum of the fans.

I wanted to leave before I started crying again. As I stepped into the mudroom I spied my glass starfish. It was covered by soot but miraculously unbroken. It sat there framed by the shattered windows. I took the starfish back to Stephen and Jane's and washed it off. Jane carefully placed it on her mantel, promising to take good care of it until our home was ready for it once again.

Alan, Griffyn and I stayed with Stephen and Jane for the first three days after the fire. We celebrated my birthday together, eating lobster and drinking lots of wine. We talked about our kids, careers and travels. As we got to know each other, conversations touched on things closer to our hearts: our dreams and, even harder to share, our fears. Occasionally, the conversation drifted back to that frightening night.

Throughout the winter we watched our house begin to rise up from the ashes. It was a very long process. Alan went back and forth to Toronto. Griffyn and I spent a few weeks at the hotel. It was comfortable, but it wasn't home.

I returned to Toronto with Alan for my mother's birthday. When it was time to return it took everything I had to leave my Ontario family once again and return to the South Shore. I wondered if the house was really worth all this sacrifice. But Alan and I had invested too much to turn back. We couldn't admit defeat. Not yet.

Slowly rooms began to take shape as windows, walls and ceilings were built and installed. It was exciting to choose paint colours, see my crown mouldings restored, have the carpets cleaned, and the hardwood floors gleaming again. Eventually, things progressed enough that Griffyn and I were able to live in the upstairs master bedroom for a few weeks until the rest of the house became habitable. Thanks goodness it had an adjoining, working bathroom.

While we lived upstairs, the main floor was still under construction. Heavy plastic covered the doorways which made it nearly impossible for heat to circulate through the rooms. My meals consisted of anything that could be microwaved or stored in the small bar fridge.

All my belongings were boxed up and stacked in the front hallway, including my kitchen things, so I used lots of paper plates and plastic cutlery. I set up a temporary dining area in the bedroom by moving the small table from the upstairs hallway and the wing-backed chair from the guest room. It was surprisingly comfortable and I ate many meals looking out at the water wondering when it would be normal again.

Stephen and Jane's home became my "go to" place for dinner or somewhere to escape from the construction. The machine that recorded our favourite television shows had been lost in the fire. I had looked forward to watching my taped Downton Abbey shows. But once again, Jane came to the rescue. She had them all taped so we watched them together, drinking tea and commenting on the characters, their clothes and their relationships.

There are those that believe things happen for a reason, and others that think life is a series of random events. A few months ago, if anyone had suggested that there could be something good that came from a house fire, I would have thought they were crazy. But now I've changed my mind. I believe that things do happen for a reason and sometimes the worst events can lead us forward in good ways.

If not for that infamous night, we might have just spent that one lovely evening having drinks and eating Chicken Bones and shortbread cookies. And, our friendship with our new neighbours might have grown slowly, over several cups of tea, and friendly nods in the grocery store, and invitations to backyard barbeques over the course of many months.

Instead, the catastrophic fire accelerated the whole process and we connected as friends and neighbours almost immediately. Looking back I see it was the right decision to move to the South Shore. Now we have a home in one of the most beautiful places in the world, and we have friends to share it with.

ABOUT VERONICA A. PURCELL

Veronica A. Purcell has spent over twenty-five years as an educator working with children and adults. Along with her husband Gerry, and Griffyn, their standard poodle, they enjoy exploring the beaches and trails around their home on the South Shore of Nova Scotia.

www.ingramcontent.com/pod-product-compliance
Lightning Source LLC
Chambersburg PA
CBHW050913120626
46552CB00004B/1553